THE ARBORIST

BY

M. S. HOLM

Sentry *Books*

Great West Publishing

USA

Sentry Books
An Imprint of Great West Publishing
Visit our Web site at www.sentrybooks.com

Copyright © 2007 by M. S. Holm
Second Edition © 2010

Library of Congress Control Number: 2007938941
ISBN Paper: 978-0-9796199-3-9
ISBN Cloth: 978-0-9796199-1-5
Illustrations by Susana Sayles
Cover artwork by Sarah Garibaldi
Book design and layout by Jonathan Gullery
Manufactured in the United States of America

CPSIA Compliance Information: Batch #0510

I

MY SISTER IRENE SAID it was the ugliest Christmas tree she had ever seen, but I didn't care. You only needed imagination to see what it could become.

I found it at the back of Mr. Paulson's tent the day my father, Irene, and I went to buy our tree. It stood by itself in the corner with its top chopped off and orange sap oozing from the end. The branches were lopsided, and the trunk was crooked. You could see white wounds where the bark had been skinned.

Irene laughed when she saw me checking it out.

"No roadkill, please," she said.

As usual, my sister had picked out the tallest tree in the tent, a perfect Douglas fir so full and triangular that it could have stood in the White House.

While my dad tied it to the roof of our minivan, I remained in the tree tent, breathing the piney smell and staring at the puny tree in the corner.

"Is this one for sale?" I asked Mr. Paulson.

"Why, it's just a lop-off, Charlie," he said. "Going to make a wreath, are you?"

"I don't know," I replied, though I knew exactly what I was going to do with it.

"Here," he said, picking it up with one hand. He held it out as if he might twirl it. "No charge."

When I carried it out of the tent, Irene protested. "Don't bring that thing near here! It's probably got tree rabies or something."

I leaned it against our car. "Trees don't get rabies," I answered.

"Dad! I don't want our tree catching whatever that sick one has!"

My dad said, "That's enough, you two. We'll put it in the back."

And that's the beauty of our Plymouth minivan. A *normal* tree fits inside.

On our way home, Irene announced, "I'm not getting within a mile of that thing."

I kept my mouth shut. The needles of my puny tree tickled me from across the rear seat. A mile was fine with me. Actually, a mile was pretty close. Irene could never have guessed that my ugly tree was going to Chief Goodyear.

I had been the first kid to spot him from the school bus when he showed up in town that September.

"Hey! Who's that?" I had said that morning, pointing to a stranger sitting on a stack of tires in the vacant lot next to Hildreth's Hardware. He was holding a pan over a fire.

In our town, you didn't see strangers cooking in public like that, so kids glued their faces to the bus windows. In the same corner of the lot, we saw a homemade tent that looked like a tepee.

"Why is he camped in our lot?" asked Gooter.

Gooter and I are best buddies, but he's a lot more territorial than me. In the summer, we played baseball and soccer in Hildreth's lot. In the winter, we built forts and waged snowball wars there.

"He must be living there," I answered.

The next day and the day after that, we saw him again. By the end of the week, rumors ran the length of the bus. Some kids said he was a hobo from the yards; others guessed he was an illegal alien. Gooter started calling him Chief Goodyear because of the tepee and his seat made of tires. Then the name stuck.

When my father drove us to church on Sunday morning, Chief Goodyear was still there. My mom noticed.

"Harold, did you see that?" she asked, looking back.

As a rule, my dad never took his eyes off the road when he was behind the wheel.

"See what?" he replied.

"A man is living in a tent next to Hildreth's."

"He's been there all week," I interjected, trying to be helpful. "I saw him from the bus."

"Maybe we should call the police," said Irene.

Of course, Irene would say something like that!

"I wonder what he's doing there," my mom remarked.

On the way home after church, my dad slowed the Plymouth in front of Hildreth's Hardware.

Chief Goodyear was busy near his tepee. His gray hair stuck out in every direction, and his clothes were dirty and rumpled like he had been sleeping in them.

Suddenly, he turned and looked at us. His face was friendly. He smiled and waved.

My parents reared back in their seats, surprised-like. You would have thought an extraterrestrial life form had waved at them. Then they lifted their hands and wagged them stiffly. I gave a big wave. Irene didn't move.

"We should report him," she whispered.

"He's not bothering anybody," I said.

"What if he's crazy? What if he's a fugitive?"

"Irene, please," said my mom.

"I wonder if he's one of the people from the hurricane," my dad muttered.

"Poor man."

"Let's get out of here," said Irene. "He gives me the creeps."

"Maybe we should help him. Bring him food or something," I suggested.

"We'll see," said my mom.

"He'll probably be gone in a few days," said my dad as we left the lot behind.

I watched Chief Goodyear return to his tent. Then I waved again.

The next week, I watched from the bus every day, expecting to see the stranger gone and our lot vacant again. The word from the back of the bus, where all the high school kids sat, was that the police were going to arrest him. Our driver said that Mr. Hildreth would run him off.

But on Friday, he was still camped in the corner, and now he had a grill. It wasn't much of a grill. It was more like a bowl with legs, but it was smoking.

"The chief is putting down roots," said Gooter. "Someone ought to tell him that's our lot."

On Saturday, I rode my Mongoose BMX to Hildreth's to buy kite string. And because I was in the neighborhood, I stopped by the lot. I just can't resist a closer look when a phenomenon is in town.

As soon as I got off my bike, I spotted the small, black dog near the tent. At first, I thought it was a stray sniffing out the chief's campsite. Then I saw it was tied to the tent.

"Hello there," I said in a friendly voice.

He gave me a perky-eared look, then lay down next to

the tent and closed his eyes. I couldn't see the stranger anywhere, though immediately I noticed how clean the lot looked. Trash had been picked up, and the big stones we used to mark corner kicks and foul lines had been gathered into piles along the walls. The area around the tent looked swept. Naturally, I wondered if the stranger had something to do with these improvements. Had Mr. Hildreth decided to put him to work instead of running him off?

Of course, I didn't think twice about giving the place a walk-around. After all, it was our lot. Mr. Hildreth had practically signed it over.

I wandered in the direction of Chief Goodyear's stack of tires. A stone held down a piece of cardboard that covered the tire holes. I held my breath and raised one corner of the cardboard, peeking in from as far away as I could. You never know what you're going to find at the bottom of a stack of tires when a man sits on them in a vacant lot. What I saw was a bag of charcoal, a sack of dry dog food, and a can of lighter fluid—not exactly what I expected, but I was relieved just the same. I let out my breath.

Nearby, the smell of burnt food reached me from the grill. I edged toward it for a closer look, but the dog suddenly jumped up and began to bark. The next moment, he was tugging on his leash in high alert.

"Not the grill," he seemed to be saying. "Not the grill!"

Then I froze. Something had stirred in the tent. Someone was inside! Before I could retreat, a pair of legs snaked from the opening. Wild, gray hair appeared, and I immediately recognized the owner.

Chief Goodyear stood. He looked at his dog and then at me.

"Shush, Pipe," he said to the dog.

"Welcome," he said to me.

"Don't talk to strangers," a little voice in my head said. It was my mom's number-one rule. Unless I wanted my picture tacked to the post office bulletin board with the word "Missing" above it, I was supposed to obey this rule while I was out and about.

"Hi, mister," I replied, just the same.

After watching him from the bus for two weeks, Chief Goodyear just didn't seem like a stranger anymore.

"I was only looking," I added quickly. I didn't want him to think that I was a spy or a stalker or someone up to no good.

The chief glanced at his tent and said, "I'm afraid there isn't much to look at."

The dog dropped his bark for a low, throaty growl. He sounded like my dad's chainsaw on idle. I watched him turn on himself, tugging at his own fur.

"Pipe, hush," the chief warned again.

The little dog stopped.

"That's a funny name for a dog," I said.

"Isn't it?" he agreed. "I pulled him from a flooded storm pipe."

Actually, Pipe looked like he had been pulled from a tar pit. His long hair was dirty and knotted and tangled with dark mud.

"A terrier is in him somewhere," said the chief, smiling. "To find it, I'll need to give him a trim and a shampoo."

I guessed a storm pipe had crossed the stranger's path, too. He looked as wild and rumpled as the first day I had seen him. He hadn't shaved, and his shoes didn't have shoelaces. He was a lot older than my dad, who gives his age as "fortysomething." The chief had gray hair and wrinkles around his eyes. Still, I liked his face. It looked kid-friendly and sort of grandfatherly. It also looked tired, like he hadn't gotten much sleep.

"Are you one of the hurricane people?" I asked.

My mom would have had a fit if she had heard me being such a busybody, but that's the way I was. The stranger didn't seem to mind my question.

He smiled. "Yes, I am."

I had seen the pictures on the television of the flattened houses, the flooding, and the people without anyplace to go.

"There was nothing left to go back to," he added. "And I didn't like where they were putting us. Pipe and I don't take much to shelters, so we came here. We needed some space."

I glanced around the lot, wondering if he needed quite this much. But I didn't say so.

"How long are you staying?" I asked.

"I guess that depends on how soon they let me go back," he said.

It sounded long-term to me. I could tell by the way he spoke that he wasn't holding his breath either.

I looked at the tent. He was right. It wasn't much to look at. It was the ugliest tepee I had ever seen. It had been put together with three different kinds of old tarpaulins. Some crooked tree limbs held it up.

"You're going to live there?" I asked, pointing to the tent.

The chief nodded. "At least for a while. Me and Pipe."

It seemed a sorry state of affairs to have to live in an ugly tepee with a dirty dog named Pipe. It was bad enough living by himself.

"Where do you go to the bathroom?"

I could see my mom's hands trying to throttle me, but the words were already out. I just had to know; we dived for pop flies and kicked soccer balls in this lot.

The chief cackled loudly. Pipe's sleepy eyelids lifted in alarm. For a moment, the laugh worried me, too. I remembered what Irene had said about him being crazy. How funny can bathroom business be?

"I go to McDonald's," he explained. "The manager lets me use the restroom there."

McDonald's was a good option. It was just around the corner.

"But you're eating here, right?" I asked, pointing to the grill.

The chief nodded again and said, "Yes, outdoor cooking is much better for you."

This was news to me. We did it just for fun at our house, and that was mostly on the weekends. I would have to tell my dad.

"Well, mister, I better get going," I said.

I had learned about as much as I needed to. He had escaped from a hurricane and found a dog in a storm pipe. He slept in a tent, used the restroom at McDonald's, and cooked outside. There was probably more to know, but I didn't want to be a pest.

"Thanks for visiting," he said as I turned toward my bike.

"Thanks for cleaning our lot," I said.

"You're welcome."

"I don't own it," I clarified, so he wouldn't think I did. "My friends and I play here sometimes."

"It's a nice lot for playing," he agreed.

Then I rode my bike home.

I didn't tell anyone about my visit.

My mom would have said, "I don't want you going back there. Do you hear me?"

My dad would have said, "Listen to your mother."

Irene would have freaked out.

I kept Gooter on the sidelines, too. I knew if I told him, he'd want to pay a visit. Then he'd want to start a game or just hang out. He'd exercise his territorial rights, and that didn't seem like a good idea, especially not with a man and his dog newly moved here from a hurricane and needing some space. So I didn't stir up anybody's anxiety.

Besides, everyone in my family was anxious enough about strangers. That next Sunday, for example, we were passing the lot on our way to church when I noticed Pipe sitting on the chief's grill. It was obvious the little dog was getting a haircut—his tangled fur finally coming off—because the chief was holding a pair of scissors. But no one else in our family had a clue.

"My God, he's eating dogs!" Irene screamed.

My dad suddenly did something he had never done before. He actually took his eyes off the road.

"Harold, should we call animal control?" my mom exclaimed.

Instantly, my dad sped up. He may have wanted to spare us the sight of blood.

I raised my voice and said, "That's his dog. He's just getting a haircut."

My dad continued to accelerate. My mom turned around to get a better view. Irene covered her eyes.

"I can't look!" she cried.

"Charlie, I think you're right," my mom agreed. "He's giving the little fellow a trim. Look, Harold."

Our Plymouth slowed and then stopped. Everyone except Irene looked back.

"How do you know it's his dog?" she demanded.

"I see him from the bus every day, that's how," I said. "The dog lives there." You have to think fast when you have a hysterical sister.

"Poor man. I wonder how he's getting by," my mom asked.

I could have answered, "Outdoor cooking." I could have said that it was better for them, too, but I kept my mouth shut. I hoped my dad would speed up again. I had never wanted to get to church so badly.

"I'm surprised he's still here," my dad said as we began to move. "The government is supposed to be helping those people."

"Maybe some of them don't like the shelters," I suggested.

The lot disappeared behind us.

Poor Pipe, I thought. Being trimmed atop an outdoor grill for everyone to see.

"I want all of us to say a prayer for him," my mom advised as we neared the church.

Under her breath, Irene muttered, "No way!"

In church, I began to wonder. That sometimes happened to me in church; between the preaching and the praying, I wondered. I wondered how the chief put milk on his cereal when he didn't have a refrigerator to keep it cold. I wondered what he used for silverware and plates. I wondered how he cooked in the rain. I wondered how he kept mosquitoes out of his tent. I wondered if he slept on the ground or on an air mattress. I wondered about his clothes, too. After all, if he wore the same ones every day, when would he get a chance to wash them?

I wondered about his money. Did he have enough to buy charcoal and dog food, but not enough for a new shirt and pants? I wondered if he had bought scissors to trim Pipe instead of razors to shave himself.

I wondered how he could feel safe at night and how he slept with the street lights on. I wondered how he did his "business" when McDonald's wasn't open.

Then I wondered about the future. What would happen when November came, the nights got cold, and the ground froze? What would become of his homemade tent when it snowed? I wondered what would happen to the chief if he caught pneumonia or got frostbite from sleeping outside.

Even for me, it was a lot of wondering.

Just before our church service ended, when the reverend asked everybody to pray for those who were sick, those on their way to heaven, and those who had already gotten there, I offered one for Chief Goodyear down the street. Of course, I knew I could do more. Prayer and wonder were only warm-ups, and something else had to be done.

Monday morning at the bus stop, Gooter said, "Let's play ball after school."

I knew what that meant. He wanted to go the lot.

Instead of coming up with an excuse not to go, like I did with my orthodontist appointment or helping my mom wash storm windows, I just played dumb.

"I don't know," I said.

I couldn't tell him that I'd already paid a visit to the lot.

"Afraid the chief is gonna scalp you, or what?" he dared.

Gooter always dared me and left little room to maneuver, unless I wanted to look like a kid who didn't believe in something impossible, like a stranger scalping two eleven-year-olds next to a hardware store. Of course, anything was possible.

"See you there," I said. If I didn't go, he'd ask Stewart or Norman or the Van Patten twins. Maybe he'd ask all of them, and that would make a crowd. Hadn't the chief said he needed some space?

When I arrived that afternoon, Gooter was already there,

tossing pop flies to himself. I noticed he was staying near the sidewalk.

"Hey, the squatter's got a dog," he whispered as soon as I pulled up. His voice made it sound like having a pet was some kind of conspiracy.

I tried to look surprised as I stared at the napping Pipe. With his fur trimmed, he was now a brown dog. The chief had revealed the terrier beneath the storm pipe. His short coat shined in the sunlight, like one of those canines in the dog food commercials.

"Maybe the guy is lonely," I suggested.

"Maybe he's staying," countered Gooter.

"Maybe," I said.

"Just so he knows this is our lot."

The tent hadn't changed since my last visit. It was still the saddest looking excuse for a tepee in our town. I wondered if the chief was stretched out inside, napping like before. If he came out and tried to recognize me, I was going to play it cool. I had my St. Louis Cardinals cap pulled down tight, giving my face plenty of shadow. In a Cardinals cap, one kid looked pretty much like another.

We edged onto the lot, tossing the ball. I felt kind of strange doing it, like I was playing in someone's backyard without permission. It felt like we were trespassing. But Gooter didn't seem to think so.

"He moved all of our stones," he complained, pointing to the piles next to the wall.

"Trash, too," I said.

I threw him a ground ball that he lifted cleanly. Without stones and trash, the fielding was easier.

"What do think is in those tires?" he asked, looking toward the stack with its cardboard cover and stone on top.

"Bathroom, maybe?" I dared.

Gooter stopped in the middle of a pitch. He made a face like he had swallowed a mouthful of sour milk. "Gross!"

"Want to check it out?"

"No way!"

Gooter immediately put some yards between himself and the chief's tires, moving to the farthest end of the lot. As soon as we spread out, he started shouting for line drives and cussing when he missed one. I knew what he was doing. He wanted to be sure the chief heard us. He was being territorial. It was pure Gooter.

But the chief didn't show. I was beginning to wonder if he was home when Gooter threw a high one that I couldn't have caught with a stepladder. The ball hit the chief's grill, then bounced hard off the tent. Pipe lifted his sleepy eyelids when it dropped near his feet.

"Nice one," I said.

"Sorry," Gooter called.

Both of us watched the tent, expecting action. I had seen it before, but this time no one stirred.

Gooter waited for me to fetch the ball, but I kneeled

to tie my sneaker instead. Wild throws belonged to the thrower. That was our rule.

"What are you waiting for?" I said finally.

Gooter approached me. His voice suddenly turned quiet. "You think he's in there?" he asked, pointing his glove at the tepee.

I shrugged. I could have said he was out scalping natives, but I resisted.

Gooter wandered to his left, trying to get a better angle on the ball. "That tent shouldn't be here anyway," he protested, still whispering.

"Get the ball," I said.

Gooter punched his glove and headed for the tent. But he only got as far as the grill.

Pipe jumped up and revved his chainsaw motor. "Not so fast," he seemed to growl.

I watched Gooter freeze. He turned to look at me. "What do I do now?" he asked.

"Stay away from the grill," I advised.

Gooter backed up, raising his hands as if Pipe had a gun. He circled wide, trying to sneak up on the tent from behind, but Pipe had him on radar now. As Gooter circled, the little dog followed him in an arc, stretching on his leash.

"He won't bite," I said, though I wasn't entirely sure of this. Pipe didn't look mean. Like Gooter, he was just territorial.

By now it was obvious that the chief wasn't in his tent. Not even a homeless person could sleep through the ruckus

Pipe was making. And to be honest, I was relieved. It's better not to find someone home if the only business you have visiting is to make him feel like he shouldn't be home. Besides, Gooter was making me nervous. He couldn't be trusted not to open his mouth and blurt something *I* would regret.

For the moment, he was busy getting our ball back while Pipe was furious with him for daring to try. The little dog pulled at his stake, following Gooter's every move and snapping at him. I couldn't help but admire the effort. It made me wonder if a storm pipe had anything to do with it. When Gooter found a stick and tried to roll the ball clear of the tent, Pipe grabbed that, too. He just wore Gooter out.

"Ah, let 'em keep it," he said finally, walking away disgusted. "I'm tired of this place!"

The truth be told, I was glad to hear Gooter say it.

That week, my mom took Irene and me to McDonald's for dinner. She does that when my dad is out of town. You may not believe this, but my dad has never stepped inside a McDonald's. It's become one of his resolutions in life to never cross the Golden Arches. My mom says his tombstone will read:

Harold Roebecker
Devoted Husband, Loving Father
Never Set Foot in McDonald's

So we were waiting in line—my mom, Irene, and I—and I was thinking what a coincidence it would be if we ran into Chief Goodyear on one of his restroom runs (McDonald's can be a small world sometimes) when suddenly I spotted him. But not where I expected. Wearing a McDonald's uniform, he was behind the counter sprinkling salt on a field of french fries.

My jaw dropped. It was definitely him, but he looked different. A hat covered his wild hair. His face seemed thinner, too. Then I realized why. The chief had shaved. He had shaved and come to work at McDonald's!

I eased behind my mom, staying out of view.

What if he recognized me? What if he said, "Hey, kid! How you doing?" What if my mom asked, "Charlie, do you know that man?" What if Irene screamed, "He's the one who eats dogs!"

This wasn't the time for introductions, so I told my mom to order me a burger and a Coke.

"No fries, dear?" she asked loudly.

I shook my head. No fries. "I'll get us a seat," I said, and then quickly disappeared into a corner booth. It was the best spot to keep out of sight until the food arrived. It was also the best place for spying. From there, I watched the chief salt and bag fries. Then I watched him go to the soft drink dispenser and push some buttons. For a new guy, he knew the terrain.

Had he worked at McDonald's before the hurricane?

When my mom came with our tray, Irene insisted we move to a window booth. She was just being contrary. As we ate, I watched her pop fries into her mouth.

If only she knew who had bagged them, I thought.

With a uniform to wear, the chief would finally have a chance to wash his clothes. Maybe he had them soaking somewhere right now. And he could bring leftovers home for Pipe. Working at McDonald's had its upside.

Then Irene said, "Charlie, get me some ketchup, would ya?"

"Why don't you get it yourself?" I replied. Obviously, I didn't want to get spotted. Besides, she had two legs.

My mom made her "you'd better be nice to your sister" face, so I got up and angled my way toward the dispensers, counting on the crowd for cover.

Please let me be just one more kid in the madhouse, I begged silently.

But the madhouse wasn't cover enough. As soon as I reached the counter and was about to grab the ketchup cups, a familiar voice caught me like a hook.

"Hey, kid! How you doing?"

The chief was replenishing the napkins and straws.

"Hi, mister," I said, trying to look surprised. "Are you working here?"

He smiled and said, "Started a few days ago. They were hiring, and I was coming here anyway."

This wasn't the time for a chat. He was working, and I was trying to get out of there.

"Well, my sister needs ketchup," I said urgently, as if Irene might go into a coma without it. "See ya."

I pumped some ketchup into a cup and ran back to the booth.

When I got there, Irene said, "What took you so long?"

She was being her usual disagreeable self. Neither she nor my mom had observed me talking to the chief. Still, I wasn't about to risk another close encounter, so I retreated to the restroom, where I washed my hands more times than I needed to. I calculated how long my mom and Irene would take to finish their food, and then I ran for the exit.

On the way home, I pondered the strange turn of events. The chief was working in a place where my dad had sworn that he would never enter. So now there were two men on the planet who would never cross paths in McDonald's.

With the chief at work, there was only Pipe to watch from the school bus windows when we passed the lot each morning. The little dog looked lonesome.

So on Saturday, I biked to Hildreth's again. But I didn't go to buy anything. This time I wanted to visit Pipe.

First, I went to McDonald's to make sure the chief was okay with my visit. It was funny how things had changed.

The week before, I had considered him to be the intruder. Now I was the one asking permission to visit the lot.

The chief was wiping tabletops near the windows.

"Hey there, kiddo," he said.

I noticed a nametag on his shirt.

"I don't even know your name," he said.

"Charlie," I replied.

The chief pointed to his nametag and said, "You can call me Bill."

Bill? Just plain Bill?

I liked Chief Goodyear better. In my house, kids didn't call adults by their first names.

"Weren't you in here last night, Charlie?" he asked.

I nodded, and he gave me a sly look.

"It's not good to eat too much fast food," he said.

"I know," I answered. I hadn't seen the movie *Super Size Me*, but Gooter had. He said it was about a guy who lived on McDonald's food for a month and nearly died from an overdose of cholesterol.

"Balance is everything," said the chief. "I see many of the same faces in here every day. Moms, dads, and kids."

I listened, thinking he didn't have to worry about my dad.

"Is it all right if I visit Pipe?" I asked.

Bill stooped to pick up the flattened remains of what looked like an Egg McMuffin.

"Sure, go ahead," he answered cheerily. "He'll be glad

for the company. I've had to leave him by himself these days, but one of us has to work. I don't want the little fellow to starve."

The chief had just released his latest economic report, but I wasn't listening. My mind was already operating in that faraway place where a kid goes when he's thinking about a dog.

"Does Pipe like chicken nuggets?"

Bill smiled and said, "Chicken nuggets will be a first for Pipe, I dare say. A new dining experience."

"Then I'll take him some."

"That's very kind of you, Charlie," he replied.

As I dug quarters out of my pockets, I decided to ask something that wasn't really my business.

"Did you work at McDonald's before you came here? You know the job really well."

He shook his head and said, "No, Charlie, I worked for a landscaper before the storm. I'm an arborist."

"What's that?" I asked.

"I take care of trees," he replied. "I plant them, prune them, and make sure they grow straight and stay healthy. I give them a better chance to live. Of course, where I come from, there aren't a lot of trees left standing now. Not a lot of anything standing."

I nodded. Being an arborist in hurricane country sounded like a risky way to make a living.

"Do you like working here?"

Bill stopped to wipe another table. "Oh, yes," he said. "It's a good meanwhile job."

"Meanwhile?" I asked.

"While I'm waiting."

"To go back? Right?"

"Yes. To go home," he said.

My mom had taught me that no one likes a spoilsport, especially one with cable television. So I kept my mouth shut about the news reports I had seen on TV. They were saying the hurricane people wouldn't be going home for months. I counted my quarters instead.

"Well, I better buy the nuggets," I said.

"Yes, of course," replied the chief. "Thanks for thinking of us, Charlie."

"Sure," I said, wondering what he meant by *us*.

I moved to the counter, where I plopped down $2.99 without even looking at the menu. I knew the price of chicken nuggets by heart.

At the lot, Pipe fired up his chainsaw growl as soon as I approached the tent. What was left of Gooter's baseball—a chewed cover and some tangled twine—were scattered near his feet.

I opened the box of nuggets, letting the smell of warm chicken hit him. The first whiff shut him up. He wagged his tail and then sat at attention like he was a dog at a state dinner.

I sat on the ground beside the tent, and Pipe sat on my lap. We renewed our acquaintance over nuggets, then over the empty box of nuggets, and finally, over my greasy, nugget-smelling fingers.

Then I peeked into Bill's tepee. Some people might have considered it snooping, but I was sitting near the entrance, so it wasn't any trouble. Inside, it looked pitiful. That's the word—pitiful.

When my dad and I went camping, we filled our tent with so much stuff there was hardly any room left for us. Air mattresses. Sleeping bags. Cookware. Canteens. Lanterns. Flashlights. A battery-operated television. Board games. We also brought enough food to feed a platoon.

Inside Bill's homemade tepee, the Grinch had come and gone, and what he'd left behind wasn't much: a lot of bare ground, a thin strip of carpet, a solitary pot, and a stack of canned goods. I recognized tuna fish and Campbell's soup. Sardines were there, too.

The sight drove a cold stake right through me, and it

wasn't because I hated sardines. I just hadn't expected to see that much bare ground. Bill was practically camped in a cave.

I stood and shook myself, still feeling that coldness inside me. My dad had said something about the government helping these people. My mom had asked us to pray. Meanwhile, an arborist without trees was working at McDonald's and living in a cave tent with canned goods and a dog he had saved from a storm pipe.

Finally, I knew what had to be done.

II

WHEN WE ARRIVED HOME with our Christmas trees that December, Irene made good on her promise to quarantine my puny pine.

"Do not bring that thing into this house," she said as our dad manhandled the big tree off the car roof and carried it to our front door.

"Mind your own business," I replied.

"The garage is the only place for it," she added. "At least we won't have to look at it there."

I had planned to take it to the garage anyway so I could fix it up, but I couldn't say that now.

"I'm going to put it on the front lawn with lights and tinsel so the whole neighborhood can see it."

"No, you won't."

"Will, too."

"Will not."

"Children," said my mom. She had come outside to watch our dad struggle with the tree. "Please, no bickering. It's almost Christmas."

"Will, too," I whispered when Irene followed my mom inside.

As a rule, I never gave Irene the last word ... not even at Christmas.

The garage was out of the question now. Putting it there would have looked like surrender, so I stood my tree on the porch instead. Then I stepped back to examine it.

Standing by itself without its piney brothers towering above it like giant sequoias, the puny tree didn't look so small anymore. In fact, it looked about the right size. Naturally, its defects remained. It was still scrawny. Its trunk was crooked, the branches lopsided, and its top hadn't made it down from Canada or wherever it had been chopped off. The orange sap and white wounds hadn't disappeared either. Still, it was perfect. The possibility was definitely there for a tree miracle.

I stood on the porch admiring it until I heard the call to come into the house. Inside, everyone was staring at Irene's perfect tree in our living room. My dad had set it up on its stand. The top almost touched the ceiling.

"What a lovely tree, Harold," bubbled my mom.

"Irene picked it out," he confessed. "She has an eye for trees."

Irene beamed like she had gotten a medal. Then she gave me her secret smirk. There was no way that I was going to let that pass.

"It looks cloned to me," I said.

The family stopped staring.

34

"What do you mean, Charlie?" my dad asked. Something in his voice wanted to know how I knew about cloning.

"It doesn't look real. It looks like it came out of a tree mold."

"Oh," he replied. "Yes ... well ... it does have a very traditional shape."

"You're just jealous," snapped Irene. "Because yours is so ugly."

My mom gave my dad a puzzled look.

"Charlie got a tree, too," he explained. "A small one."

"A sick, midget tree," added Irene. "It got puked from the forest."

"That's enough," my mom said.

"Irene's tree took steroids," I shot back. "It looks like the Arnold Schwarzenegger of Christmas trees."

"Dad!"

Our dad raised both hands and said, "Okay, you two, get ready for supper. And no more discussion of trees. Each of you got the one you wanted, so both of you should be happy."

As Irene retreated to the kitchen, she said, "At least my tree is in the house."

I had a comeback ready, but I stopped myself. What I wanted to say couldn't be said without tipping my hand.

Sure, her tree was in the house, and mine wasn't. Sure, her tree stood tall while mine looked puny. And yes, her tree was full, and mine was scrawny. But, like so many other Christmas trees, hers was standing in an ordinary living room while mine was going to stand somewhere special. But I couldn't say it.

For the first time, I let Irene have the last word.

A long time ago, Irene was actually normal. She was even nice. Not sweet; I don't overdo my adjectives. I'd just say she was nice, maybe even normal-nice. She would laugh every time I did something stupid. She actually used my name, too. Sometimes she even gave me compliments like, "Awesome look, Charlie," the day I wore my Hawaiian shirt to give an oral report at school.

Nowadays, she didn't call me Charlie. ("Is *he* coming too?") Instead of compliments, I got complaints and threats. ("Better not, or I'll tell Mom.") When I'm not invisible, I'm just a "bug-eyed creep."

Though it seemed like ancient history now, there was a time when my sister was fun to be around. On car trips, she would read me Shel Siverstein, and we'd laugh at the crazy pictures. Also, she would do an impersonation of our Aunt Marion that left me rolling on the floor. Whenever I asked her to do to it now, she told me to get lost.

In the old days, Irene was generous, too. She'd give me her leftover fries at McDonald's. She'd share her Halloween loot. She'd let me listen to her music, and once, she loaned me her CD player for a Boy Scout trip. She even participated

in a five-kilometer run for some boys in Sudan. She didn't even know the boys, but she ran for them.

Now she wore a T-shirt that summed up her stinginess. It said, "It's all about me!" She wore it at least twice a week. I sometimes thought she did it just to bother me.

My mom said Irene was going through a phase. She said that I would go through it, too, but I didn't think so. I could never be that stingy. Even Gooter, who was territorial and a poor loser, would give away half his lunch if yours fell out of a locker and ended up at the bottom of a stampede at recess. Compared to Irene, Gooter was Mother Teresa.

So how could I expect her to understand that a homeless man needed a Christmas tree, even if it was a puny Christmas tree without a top? How could I expect her to be nice? Being generous and nice had belonged to the other Irene, the one before the T-shirt. Living with the sister I had now was like living with a stranger.

When I left Bill's tent that Saturday morning in October, I knew exactly where I was headed. I went straight to the bottom shelf of my mom's linen closet where she stored our bedding.

The sight of that thin carpet stretched on the bare ground kept replaying in my head like a bad music video. First I saw the chief lying on it, tossing and turning. Then I saw him lying under it, tossing and turning. Next I saw him trying to roll up in it.

I couldn't imagine anyone sleeping on the ground without a blanket or a pillow, so I grabbed one of each from the linen closet. I borrowed a pillowcase, too. Then I snatched two facecloths and a couple hand towels. We had plenty of both.

Remaining out of sight in the garage, I tied everything onto my bike rack. Then a better idea came to me. I'd let the chief have my mummy bag. With cold nights coming, he needed it more than I did. Besides, my parents had promised me a new one for my birthday.

I spotted my dad's foam ground pad, the one that had touched the soil of seven continents (Antarctica might have been a stretch) when he was younger. All that traveling had worn out both of them, which is to say the pad had patches, and my dad didn't hop continents anymore. He wouldn't mind giving it to a good cause. The point was to get Bill off the ground.

Fortunately, Saturday mornings at our house were ideal for prowling in the closets. Irene slept until noon, and even then, she begged for overtime. My mom always did the grocery shopping, and my dad went to his Army Reserve meetings twice a month.

Still, eyes were watching outside. Mrs. Simon, our nosy widow neighbor, always had her face in the window, and Mr. Hatch, our chatty mailman, usually appeared precisely at the wrong moment. Once, he even caught me answering nature's urgent call behind the oleanders. Either of these two might phone my mom to ask why I was exiting the house with a pillow, towels, and a sleeping bag tied to my bike. Was I running away from home? So I pedaled like crazy once I left the garage.

When I got to the lot, I did a quick ride-by to make sure the chief wasn't back from McDonald's. Then I parked my bike next to the tepee. Pipe didn't growl. Instead he wagged his tail and searched for chicken nuggets. He sniffed every-where, but he only picked up the scents of laundry soap, musty garage, and the soil of seven continents. As usual, the area around the tent was swept. The chief sure kept a clean campsite.

I piled the bedding and towels inside the tent, making sure they were out of Pipe's reach, and then I biked home. I didn't want any of our lot gang to see me, especially Gooter. I also didn't want the chief to know who had been there. Some people don't take charity well. They don't see it for what it really is: the chance to give away something you don't need anymore.

The following week, we visited my grandmother in Huntsville. The next weekend, my mom took Irene and me to shop for winter coats at the factory outlets in Jefferson, which was a waste of a perfectly good weekend.

When my first free Saturday came around, I gathered a few more essentials for the chief, including a flashlight with batteries and a saucepan my mom had put in the box for the Salvation Army. I added a few pieces of silverware, too, and because it was still a mystery what the chief used for dishes, I threw in a mug, a dinner plate, and a soup bowl. All were taken from the deepest corners of our kitchen cupboards.

I packed everything in a large pail, which was also going to the cause. Every campsite needs a pail—for water, laundry, dishwashing, or just sitting. It had to be more comfortable than tires.

Pretending not to remember me, Pipe started growling when I got there. Then I unwrapped a stuffed pork chop taken from our refrigerated leftovers. That cured his amnesia.

I felt better when I looked inside the tent this time. The stuff left from my first trip had found a home. The sleeping bag was stretched across my dad's foam ground pad. The pillow was tucked in the opening. My mom's towels were folded neatly. And the thin strip of carpet had become Pipe's new bed.

I waited another week before I visited McDonald's. The chief was busy on the drive-through lane when I arrived, so I rode my bike around to the window.

"Hey, Charlie," he said, looking surprised. "I think this is supposed to be for cars."

"It's okay," I replied. "The sign doesn't say so. I just wanted to know if I can visit Pipe again."

"Sure, you can walk him if you want. I didn't have a chance this morning."

"*No problema*," I answered, practicing my Spanish vocabulary like Señora Burns, my teacher, always suggested.

"A walk around the lot will be fine. Just keep him on his leash. Okay?"

"*Bueno.*"

"And don't worry about his little deposits. I'll pick those up."

"Sounds fair," I said, switching back to English. I hadn't come prepared to discuss dog deposits in another language.

Bill smiled, but his face soon turned quizzical.

"I've been wanting to ask. Have you seen anyone visiting my tent?"

I was ready for it, so I said, "Just me, when I went to see Pipe."

That was the carefully worded truth. I tried to look interested, but not too interested.

Bill nodded and said, "Someone has been leaving me things like towels and dishes. Even a sleeping bag. I thought you might know something about it."

He was looking at me with the x-ray stare that adults use when they want to read the truth behind your eyes. Another kid might have blinked. Not me.

"A lot of charitable people live in this town," I offered. "When that tsunami hit last year, our church filled a whole tractor trailer with stuff to send. A lot of sleeping bags were in it." I stopped because you never want to say too much about charity.

Bill nodded gravely. "Yes, I know. I gave some blankets, too. It was a natural disaster of catastrophic proportion."

He was still looking at me, but the x-ray gaze was gone. I was impenetrable. Fortunately, tsunamis have a way of detouring a conversation.

Cars were backing up in the drive-through lane. I watched the chief shift gears and go back to work.

"What will it be, Charlie? Nuggets again?"

"Nothing," I said. "I'm taking your advice about not eating so much fast food."

"Oh."

"I just wanted to check about going to see Pipe. That's all."

"Thank you, Charlie."

His McDonald's voice had returned. It was time for me to pull ahead.

"*Adios.*"

At the lot, I walked Pipe on his leash. He was like one of those dogs in prison camp movies, patrolling the perimeter. But those dogs didn't ever stop to mark the walls or leave deposits, so I guessed Pipe would never go to Hollywood.

I was tying him back to his stake when a voice called out from the sidewalk.

"Roebecker, you dog thief!"

When I looked up, I saw Gooter jumping off his bike.

I tried not to look like it was a big deal. Gooter and I were best buddies because we had a lot in common. We had snooty sisters and trouble with fractions. We didn't like green vegetables, and we showed up in places when we were not supposed to. Gooter said it was because we lived in a small town where boys looking for the extraordinary were naturally going to run into each other. And in our town, there definitely wasn't a whole lot of extraordinary.

I took my time making sure that Pipe's leash was tied tightly. I secretly hoped he would remember Gooter from his last visit and fire up some fury.

Pipe locked on him, growled for a second, and then gave a welcoming wag of his tail, as if Gooter were an old friend. I stared, not quite believing it.

"That stupid dog owes us a baseball," Gooter said.

"I think he ate it," I replied. The cover and twine were nowhere to be seen.

"What are you tying him up for?"

"So he won't run away."

"Let him run away. Then we can play."

I couldn't tell if Gooter was kidding or not. He sometimes took a joke to the edge.

"I can't. It's not our dog."

Gooter looked around the lot. "Are you snooping or what?" he asked.

44

"Sort of. I went to McDonald's and then I rode by." Both true.

"Every time I come, the guy is never around," said Gooter.

I didn't offer any explanations. Obviously, he didn't know that the chief was working at McDonald's.

"What are *you* doing here?" I asked. I wanted him to know that I wasn't the only one without any business in the neighborhood.

Gooter shrugged and said, "Just keeping an eye on things. Hey, it's still our lot."

Gooter was being territorial again. He moved to the tepee entrance, bending to look inside.

"Man, he's got dishes and stuff in here. Look!"

I knew I shouldn't. It wasn't the same as dropping off charity. But I stuck my head in anyway. I tried to seem curious, but I hoped no one would see us. Also, I didn't want Gooter recognizing my mummy bag from Sean Miller's sleepover the year before.

"Looks pretty poor to me," I said, backing out.

"Yeah. Like in Africa."

Gooter was always connecting to Africa—due mostly to his mother who made him watch the National Geographic channel.

"I bet it's no fun living here," I remarked.

"My dad says he's from the hurricane."

"I heard that, too," I said. I could have added that I heard it from the chief himself, but I was watching my words.

Gooter studied the grill.

"I want to feel sorry for him," he said. "It's a bad deal getting run off by a hurricane, but I wish he'd picked another place to camp."

"I guess some people need space," I said. "Mr. Hildreth hasn't made him leave."

"Yeah, but Fuzzy Jergon just got a new soccer goal—you know, the portable kind—and he was going to bring it to the lot, but when I told him about losing our ball, he said his dad would kill him if something happened to the net."

"Maybe we'll have to pick another place to play," I said. "Until he leaves."

"How much longer is that going to be? It's almost Halloween."

"Halloween doesn't have anything to do with it," I said. "He's just waiting for the water to go down or whatever so he can go home."

Gooter seemed to consider this.

I added, "The best thing we can do is be Christian about it. Imagine having all your stuff underwater. It must be awful. At least he has dry ground here."

"I suppose," Gooter agreed, his voice sounding less territorial than usual. "But he should go to the bathroom someplace else. That's gross." He pointed to the stack of tires with its cardboard cover.

I said, "It's not his bathroom, Gooter. I checked it out. Come on."

I headed toward the tires, but he hung back. When I removed the cardboard and stuck my hand in the hole, Gooter's eyes bugged out as if he had bitten into a jalapeño straight out of the can. Then he saw me lift out the bag of charcoal.

"Dude!" he cried, running to see for himself. "That is so not cool," he said with relief in his voice.

I couldn't tell him everything I knew, but I could tell him what was most important.

"The chief's not messing with our lot, Gooter. He's just trying to get by."

Gooter stared at the contents of the tire hole.

"Yeah," he said. "I see what you mean."

At school, they gave us donation boxes to carry with our trick-or-treat bags on Halloween—so people could give money for the hurricane victims. It seemed like a good idea. That night, trick-or-treating on our street, I filled my box in the first hour, which goes to show that a lot of generous people live in our neighborhood. The next morning at the breakfast table, as I stared at the words "Hurricane Victims" on the donation box, I got another idea.

Why shouldn't I give my box to the chief, our very own hurricane victim, and save the trouble of sending it off? I could ask Gooter to add his box too, and we could deliver them to the chief ourselves.

When I mentioned my idea to Gooter, he didn't like it.

"That's stealing, Charlie," he said.

"No it's not," I replied. "The money is for the victims. We're just delivering it."

"We're only supposed to collect it," he said. "Besides, the boxes are numbered. We have to return them empty or full."

He was right. But did a donation box have to be only empty or only full?

"How about if we take half the money out, give it to the chief, then turn the other half in?" I might not be good at fractions, but I still knew the basics.

Gooter stared at me like I was crazy. "Dude, do you want to go to jail?"

That scared me because Gooter doesn't usually use jail as an excuse not to do something. So that was the end of it. I turned in my box, and he did, too.

In November, people started raking leaves and wearing coats. Kids on the bus didn't pay attention to Hildreth's lot anymore. The chief's campsite became something ordinary on our route, like pumpkins on doorsteps. Our soccer games relocated to Fuzzy Jergon's backyard, and Gooter stopped his territorial talk of taking over the lot.

On our drive to church every Sunday, I always turned to see if the chief was on the lot. Naturally, Irene never wasted an opportunity to voice her opinion.

"I don't understand why you keep looking at that horrible place," she'd say.

For the next two weekends, my dad kept me busy around the house with yard work. I had to rake and bag leaves. Then I had to carry the bags and empty them. Even Irene had to help, which was some consolation because she hated leaves.

Though I didn't have a chance to visit the lot or McDonald's, I still prowled our closets looking for items to take to the chief. I also inspected the Salvation Army box more thoroughly, where I discovered some great stuff, including a teakettle without a cover that would work for boiling water. There was my dad's cardigan pullover sweater that he never wore—blue elephants on beige weren't his style—and there was also a pair of gardening gloves that would keep the chief's hands warm. I found a handheld mirror he could use for shaving, as well as some treasures from a bygone era, including an old thermos, a knit ski hat from when my parents lived in Vermont, and a pocket sewing kit with patches and four different-colored threads. I also found the bedpan from when my grandfather had lived with us and couldn't climb the stairs, but I didn't take it. Even charity has its limits.

When I was done, my backpack was bulging. I even made room for two cans of Hormel Chili and a pair of men's woolen

socks that I pulled from a box marked "church rummage sale."

I didn't have a chance to deliver anything until Veteran's Day. With school out, my dad in the parade, and my mom on the VFW refreshment committee, it was the perfect chance to escape. But Bill was home when I arrived.

I started to ride past the lot, but he saw me.

"Hey, Charlie," he called out.

I waved as if I was in a hurry to go somewhere else, but his invitation tested my good manners.

"Come over and say hi to Pipe," he called.

I left my bike at the curb and dropped the backpack to the ground.

At the tent, Pipe immediately sniffed me over. In return, I gave him a rowdy face-cuddle.

"Pipe is getting spoiled," said the chief, chuckling. "Chicken nuggets *and* canned cat food. Can you believe it? That charitable person left four cans. Pipe likes them so much that he doesn't want to eat the dry dog food anymore."

I tried to chuckle too, but I'm not good at it. The truth was I hadn't brought any cat food to the tent.

"I sure would like to know who that person is," the chief mused, giving me another of those x-ray looks.

I noticed a shopping bag behind Pipe. I wanted to move the conversation along, so I asked, "Did you visit the mall?"

He shook his head. "No, the charitable soul left that, too.

Two brand new pairs of socks still in their package. I found them when I got back."

If I had been on the chief's list of suspects, the surprise on my face instantly cleared me of suspicion. And I wasn't faking.

"New stuff, huh?" I said, glancing at the sidewalk where my backpack remained with those used socks from the rummage sale box. So I wasn't the only one on a charitable mission.

"You were right about the generous people in this town, Charlie. I guess someone must think I'm staying for the winter."

My mind darted through a briar patch of possibilities. A charitable mom? Someone on the bus? Gooter?

Gooter's dad owned a clothing store, but Gooter didn't have a cat. It was probably someone I didn't know.

"Whoever it is, I sure do appreciate it," continued the chief. "But I hope to be out of here by Christmas."

I started listening again.

"Are you going back home?"

"Not that soon. They're still pumping out the water from where I lived. No one is going to be let back for months."

If he was keeping up on current events, it wasn't necessary for me to hold back on the grim outlook.

"On the TV, they're saying you won't be going back for years," I said.

"I'm going to Florida," continued the chief. "It's warmer there."

"Florida?"

I wanted to say that hurricanes liked warm weather, too, but I figured he already knew that.

"I might have a better chance there of finding the kind of work I do," he added.

I nodded. "Being an arborist, right?"

"Yes, you remembered."

"It's not an easy word to forget," I replied.

"No, it's not," he agreed.

"I like trees, too," I added, which was true. I just didn't like raking their leaves.

The chief smiled and said, "I'm glad to hear it, Charlie. Trees can teach us a lot about surviving and getting through the hard times. They are a lot tougher than most of us think. We can learn a lot from them."

This was news to me. I mostly liked the way they looked and the sound their leaves made in the wind. Their shade was cool, too.

"I hope you find that kind of job," I said. Trees in Florida would be lucky to have the chief in their state.

"Thank you, Charlie. Me, too. But first I have to save up some more money before I fold camp. It's two of us traveling now."

I looked at Pipe and I thought, "You're one lucky dog. This man is going to take care of you like a tree!"

That was the end of our conversation. I had to catch the end of the parade, and he had to work the lunch shift.

"See ya!" I said.

The chief followed me to the edge of the lot and watched me put on my backpack. Naturally, I wanted to make a quick getaway.

"What do you have in there?" he asked, pointing to the pack with its load of undelivered items.

I couldn't say books because it wasn't a school day.

"Just stuff," I answered, trying to sound like a kid without a vocabulary.

"I was reading about a study the other day," continued the chief. "It said kids are putting too many books in their packs. It's not good for you."

I nodded. He had said the same thing about fast food.

"I'll lighten it up," I said, riding off on my bike.

And I did. The next week, I lightened it up inside Bill's tent—leaving him everything except that pair of rummage sale socks. My sole witness was Pipe—the only dog on the planet who was as lucky as a tree.

As Thanksgiving neared, I found myself flirting with the idea of inviting the chief to our house for turkey dinner. But the more I thought about it, the more it seemed to be a tricky proposition. First, I'd have to go public with our acquaintance. Next, my parents would have to agree to the invite. (I could hear Irene shrieking, "Invite *who?*") Finally, the chief would have to accept.

When I imagined what his Thanksgiving would be like, the picture wasn't a pretty one. I saw him on the lot, sitting lonesome-like on his pail, hunched over a Big Mac or a warmed-up can of Hormel Chili while our family feasted on turkey with all the fixings, everyone waiting for the gravy to be passed. It didn't seem right. That cold stake got stuck inside me again.

So one evening at dinner, I tested the waters. My mom mentioned that my Uncle Will, Aunt Marion, and their kids might drive from Rockdale for the holiday.

"If people don't have a family, what do they for Thanksgiving?" I wondered aloud.

"People without family often go somewhere," replied my mom smoothly.

"Like a restaurant?" I ventured.

"Or friends invite them to dinner. Some may cook at home, too."

She had used the right word—the *home* word.

"And the homeless? They don't have a place to cook. What about them?"

My dad asked for the potatoes and then fielded my question.

"There are places that serve dinners, son. Rescue missions. Community soup kitchens."

I had heard of these places. "Like breadlines?" I asked.

Their forks stopped moving.

"Not exactly," said my mom. "People actually sit down to eat, dear. They get a complete meal."

"Where did you hear about breadlines?" my father asked, eyeing me over the bowl of potatoes.

"In social studies. We've been reading about the Great Depression."

They nodded and resumed eating. I was tempted to add that some folks were caught in a depression just as great today, but I left that to history.

My mom said, "This year, the ladies at the Safe Harbor Hospitality House are sponsoring a Thanksgiving dinner for the needy at the Crossroads Shelter. I'll be baking some pies."

That doesn't sound bad … if they get pie.

"What about inviting someone to your house?" I asked.

My parents gave me puzzled looks.

"What do you mean?" inquired my dad while he served himself broccoli.

"I mean inviting a homeless person for Thanksgiving dinner. Do people do that?"

"No way! Don't even go there, mister!" exclaimed Irene. "I don't want any stranger coming into our house. He could kill the whole family."

My dad swallowed swiftly and said, "Irene, those kinds of comments aren't necessary. I think you're watching too many movies."

It warmed my heart to hear it. I gave her my "Dad sure got you" smile.

"I bet you want to invite that creepy guy from the tent, don't you?" Irene said.

Sometimes, mostly by accident, Irene got it right. She was dangerous in that way.

"What creepy guy?" I asked, innocent-like, not missing a forkful of meatloaf. I had to stay cool.

"You know who I mean. That man at Hildreth's. You're always looking at him when we drive by there. I've seen you on the bus."

"I've seen you staring at Billy Wetmore on the bus," I countered, "but I'm not making a big deal out of it."

"Billy Wetmore? What do you mean?" she said, playing dumb. But her face revealed the truth. "I look at a lot of people. So?"

"Same here," I said. "But I don't ogle them."

Such a sorry sight just had to be reported.

"That's enough," said my dad, using his army voice. "Everyone eat."

Only the clicking of forks and the slurping of milk filled the silence that followed.

"As a rule, we don't invite people we don't know into our home, Charlie," advised my mom quietly. "It just isn't done … unless there is an emergency or something like that."

Emergency? A homeless arborist working at McDonald's

and living in a homemade tent with winter coming. Wasn't that an emergency?

For a moment, I debated if I should tell them everything. Then I decided against it. I had tested the family waters, and they were as cold as where the Titanic had sunk. Besides, I couldn't let Irene know she had guessed right about my stares from the bus window. I would never have the last word again.

The chief would have to settle for a Thanksgiving dinner sponsored by the Safe Harbor Hospitality House at the Crossroads Shelter.

Still, I dared a last stab at particulars.

"If homeless people don't have phones or mailboxes, how do they hear about the free turkey and pie?"

My mom smiled. She wore the same smile whenever she stood in the Women's Auxiliary booth serving coffee cake for the hospital benefit.

"We publicize, dear. We put it in the paper and on the radio. We put up posters, and we give flyers to the merchants."

"Like McDonald's?"

My mom frowned. "No, I don't think so. Fast-food chains have rules about local advertising. Don't they, Harold?"

"Don't ask me about McDonald's," my dad replied. "It's an alien planet as far as I'm concerned."

"I'm sure you'll see one at school," my mom said.

And she was right. The next week, a sign announcing the Thanksgiving dinner at the Crossroads Shelter was tacked to the community service bulletin board next to the gym lockers at school. When no one was looking, I took it down and stuffed it in my backpack. The afternoon before Thanksgiving I delivered it to the chief's tent together with a bag of mixed nuts. There had been two bags in our pantry, but when my uncle and aunt had canceled on us, I figured we could get by with one. And just in case the complete dinner my mom had raved about would be missing the side dish most deserving of Pilgrim gratitude, I also left the chief a can of cranberry sauce.

I set the nuts and sauce next to his brand-new socks that were still in their package, but the sign for the Thanksgiving dinner I left on the chief's pillow—so he couldn't lie down without reading it. I never knew if he went.

Those first weeks in December, I supplied the chief with soap, Band-Aids, toothpaste, and toilet paper. Also Advil and Alka-Seltzer. We had plenty of both at our house.

I left pretzels, power bars, bottled water, and the most recent issues of *Time* magazine. My dad never read them anyway. I brought candles, matches, and extra batteries for the flashlight. I delivered packets of cocoa, envelopes of instant oatmeal, and a box of teabags—food to keep the chief warm. And I even dropped off some vitamins, so he wouldn't get sick.

I kept an eye open for that other charitable person, but I never saw anyone else on the lot. That was a relief since charity is better if it's anonymous.

I still wondered if it might be Gooter, so one day on the bus, without any warm-up to the subject, I asked, "Have you been by the lot?"

Gooter shook his head. "My dad has me working at the store unpacking clothes for the Christmas rush."

"Socks?" I asked, watching his face.

"Yeah, socks," he answered wearily. "About a zillion. Why?"

"Just wondering," I said. "In case I need a pair."

He didn't give away anything except the fact that he was tired of packaged clothing. It was hard to say if he was playing dumb.

By the fifteenth, the weather got chilly. As I ran to catch the bus one morning, our front lawn crunched under my feet. When I looked down, I saw that the brown grass was stiff with frost. I thought about the chief lying inside his sleeping bag with only a foam pad between him and the cold ground. I wondered if he would finally leave for Florida.

On the day that school let out for the holidays, I went straight to McDonald's. I needed to know if he was staying for Christmas.

To my surprise, I saw him sipping coffee at a table when I

arrived. Christmas decorations hung on the window behind him, and holiday music played from the speakers. The chief needed only a newspaper to look like a regular customer.

When he saw me with my Oreo McFlurry, he waved and said, "Hey, Charlie. Sit down. You caught me on break."

I sat down and sucked hard on my straw.

"If you've come to see Pipe, I'm afraid you won't find him home," he said. "I've put him in a shelter."

"A shelter?" I repeated, suddenly getting a brain freeze. It was part shock, part ice cream.

The chief lifted a finger and said, "Don't worry. He's fine. With the cool weather, I decided he would be better off under a roof, so I boarded him at the humane society. Don't you think it would be cruel to leave him outside this time of year?"

Actually, I hadn't thought about it. As soon as I did, I knew he was right. The same thing could be said about people sleeping outside, too.

"Yeah, we got frost at our house on Thursday," I said.

"It has been nippy in the mornings," he agreed. "When I feel cold, I get some coffee." He lifted his cup to show me. "But Pipe has to depend on others for help." He shook his head. "Let me tell you. It's tough having to depend on others."

I knew he was right. As a kid, I was the definition of dependent. It wasn't easy.

But I also had heard, mostly in church, that depending

was part of living together. And I'm not just talking about dogs and people.

"Poor fellow," mused the chief. "I miss him already. He didn't like the move. New scenery. New company. New smells. He had to have his shots so he could stay. He was not a happy camper when I left him, but neither of us is much for shelters."

"Is that because they're crowded and smelly?" I asked. I had heard this somewhere, probably on TV.

"Yes, Charlie, some are. Shelters can be very good places, too, for people who need protection. But I'm an outdoor person and kind of independent. When something like this happens, when you lose everything you own, you need to be around whatever makes you feel better."

"Like trees and space, right?"

The chief nodded. "You might say that."

I thought about what he had just said. It was scary to even think about losing everything.

"You weren't able to grab some clothes or a clock radio or anything when your house flooded?"

"No, Charlie. The water came up too fast, and I waited too long to leave. It's hard to leave your home."

I knew. I had run away once when my mom had thrown out my dead bird collection without asking permission. As soon as I had left, I wanted to come back, which I did eventually. But first I walked to the edge of town and sat under a tree for three hours. There really was no place like home.

"Don't you have a family or friends or someone?" I asked. It was none of my business, but I had been wondering about his family for some time.

The chief smiled, but he didn't look like he was happy. "I have a sister, but we don't stay in touch. We haven't spoken for years."

"I've got a sister," I said. "And it's been years since we've been in touch."

"My sister is a very good person," said the chief.

"Mine is selfish and mean."

"That will change," he said.

"Not soon enough."

"When it comes to family, Charlie, especially sisters, you can't miss the forest for the trees. None of us is perfect. If you see only what you don't like about her, then you will miss seeing the things you do. That's a shame because those are the things that will bring you together and keep you a family, even when you're apart."

I had never understood that saying about the forest for the trees. With an arborist using it now to talk about family, I was really confused.

"For the present, my only family is Pipe," added the chief. "And even he is living away from me now."

"At least he'll be warm," I volunteered.

"Yes. And it's only until we leave. I'm taking the little fellow with me. As much as we've been through together, I couldn't go without him."

"So you're leaving before Christmas?" I asked.

He drank the last of his coffee. "Probably not. Pipe's shots and his boarding set me back a bit, so I'm going to work another week or two. There's a chance for some overtime because my coworkers want time off during the holidays. That'll help. I have nothing else to do over Christmas. I might as well work."

Holiday music still played from the speakers. I looked at customers eating their burgers and fries. I looked at kids running around. None of them knew how close they were to a homeless man who lived in a tent and served fast food to pay for dog shots.

"That doesn't sound like much of a holiday," I said. "Working on Christmas and not even having Pipe."

The chief smiled and looked at his watch. He said, "Charlie, that's life. Sometimes, you have to bend in the wind."

He was talking about trees again. Both of us stood up.

"Well, I have to get back to work," he said.

"Yeah, I better head home."

"Nice chatting with you, Charlie."

"Say hi to Pipe for me," I said as I left, satisfied with my fact-finding. The chief was definitely staying for the holidays.

And that's when I decided to find a Christmas tree and put it next to his tent. A man who took care of his dog better than he took care of himself deserved a tree. So did an arborist who had to work at McDonald's on Christmas.

III

WHEN MY MOM SAW my puny tree, she forgot the true spirit of Christmas and lied.

"Charlie, it's so cute!" she exclaimed.

"Think so?" I replied.

"I see wonderful possibilities here for a wreath."

Mr. Paulson had said the same thing, but he didn't say "wonderful possibilities." My mom had other ideas, too.

"Maybe we could take some boughs and make a beautiful centerpiece for the table. Or, here's a thought. Why don't we put pine needles around the crèche this year?"

Pine needles around our crèche? "Hello!" I almost blurted. "Jesus wasn't born anywhere near a pine tree!"

Setting up our crèche was one of the few things I still did with my mom at Christmas. Each year, I positioned the key players, including Mary, Joseph, and the inconsiderate innkeeper. My mom took care of the livestock, angels, and gawking shepherds. Early Christmas morning, I dropped the baby Jesus into his manger while she made sure the straw was there to catch him. Over the next twelve days, I moved the magi toward the stable, and with me at the

wheel, they definitely took the long route. My mom, meanwhile, made sure I didn't park them before Epiphany. She said that having a crèche was a way for us to stay in touch with the true meaning of Christmas. She said people often forgot the miracle.

My mom always talked like that around the holidays, but now she wanted pine needles in the desert. Talk about miracles!

"Mom, I don't want to chop it up," I said about my tree. "I'm going to do something special with it." I didn't want to get more specific than that.

"Of course, dear," she said. "It's your tree. Just make sure you get it in some water so it won't dry out."

My mom had advice for everything. Most of it was good.

"If you plan on leaving it outside," she added, "please take care what you use for decorations. Things seem to be disappearing around here lately. Irene says that one of Trudy's bowls was taken from the porch last week."

Trudy was Irene's pampered cat. She used to have two bowls, but the week before I had given one of them to Pipe. A cat didn't needed two bowls anyway.

"I'll keep an eye out for it," I replied. And I would.

"I just don't understand people," said my mom, shaking her head. "Christmas should be a time of giving, not taking. If you ask me, the world is an upside-down place."

I didn't say anything, but I knew she was right. A world where an arborist had to work at McDonald's to support himself and his dog while living in a homemade tent was definitely an upside-down place.

Before my tree went to the lot, I knew it would need a major makeover if it was to pass for a presentable evergreen. Grown-ups like to say that beauty is in the eye of the beholder. For a kid, ugly is always right there where you can see it.

So I borrowed my mom's rosebush clippers and carefully pruned the piney edges. On any Christmas tree, trimming is a tricky business, but on a scrawny one, it's like reading your sister's diary without her permission. As soon as you start, you want to stop.

I couldn't do anything about the crooked trunk or the missing top, but I picked away the gummy, orange ooze where the bark had been skinned. And I put plenty of sugar in the tree water. My grandfather used to say that sugar was the best way to make a Christmas tree forget it doesn't have roots.

I thought of the chief as I fixed up the little tree, wondering if my work would meet his approval. Just my luck, the guy was an arborist. And not just any arborist. He was an arborist who said trees were his teachers.

Why couldn't he have been a car salesman or a house painter?

When it was time to decorate, I resisted borrowing from our own tree. Irene watched over our Christmas ornaments like they were the crown jewels. She even knew how many blinking bulbs were in the light sets. She personally took charge of positioning every sphere and every star on every limb, as if the gravitational balance of the universe depended upon it. Einstein would have laughed. I know I did. There wasn't any way that I was going to sneak away with a major ornament.

So I settled for a handful of tinsel and the candy canes from my mom's mantle arrangement of angels looking down on Santa Claus in his sled. Believe me, candy canes didn't add anything to it. I popped two bags of microwave popcorn, which I strung together on several yards of dental floss. After that, I threaded a garland of elbow macaroni. Then I found some construction paper and made a couple paper chains.

For the next two days, I worked as hard as any of Santa's elves. I gilded pinecones and glued glitter on acorns. I made clothespin reindeer and pipe-cleaner church bells. I constructed stars out of Popsicle sticks, and I cut Christmas trees from red felt. With the leftover yellow paint from my go-cart, I coated a dozen light bulbs. I wrapped aluminum foil on Styrofoam balls, wired seashells, and readied frozen orange juice lids for hanging with fish hooks. When it seemed that my collection of ornaments was missing something modern, I added a couple of my CDs, which were scratched from the days when I played too many video games. For the treetop, I found a cardboard angel left over from a Christmas pageant. I wrapped it in plastic sandwich wrap to make it look glossy,

and then I glued it to an empty toilet paper tube for support. No angel was more down-to-earth.

When my mom observed my elaborate preparations, she said, "That's going to be quite a tree, dear. Have you decided where you're putting it?"

"Someplace," I answered, maintaining the mystery as politely as I could. After all, I couldn't really say that it was none of her business.

"Not around here," interrupted Irene.

My mom corrected her. "Irene, Charlie can put his tree wherever he chooses."

Irene rolled her eyes while I smiled. Mom had just silenced my sister, and I had just gotten the green light to move my tree wherever.

But the road to wherever had a pothole ahead. I had to get a fully decorated Christmas tree out of our house, past the neighbors, across town, and onto Hildreth's lot. Conjugating a Spanish verb in three tenses seemed easier.

I considered the options. First, I could transport it— without any ornaments—by bike, and then decorate it at the lot. But even if I managed to decorate the tree in record time, half the town would recognize me.

"Hey, isn't that the Roebecker boy over there hanging CDs on that poor excuse for a tree?" people would say.

The second option was to deliver the tree, leave off the ornaments, and let the chief do the decorating. But that was like getting a Christmas card from your grandparents without any money inside. What kind of gift-giving was that?

Option three was to boldly go where no boy on a bicycle had gone before. And that meant delivering one upright Christmas tree already assembled and ready to admire.

Was there really any other choice for a kid who wanted to make a difference in the world?

It was a nerve-tingling marvel to behold a fully loaded pine tree sitting atop my Mongoose BMX in the dimly lit secrecy of our garage on Christmas Eve morning. The sight of it tied to the steering tube with its crooked trunk wired to the handlebars gave me some serious goose bumps. I wondered if the first American in space had felt this way just before launch. Had he been tempted to call the whole thing off, shimmy down the gantry, and go back to bed?

But the countdown had begun. If I didn't deliver it now, while my parents and Irene were out fighting the crowds of last-minute shoppers, and while the chief was serving breakfast at McDonald's, then history would not be made.

Still, I hesitated.

Did making history have to be quite so obvious?

Then in one of those flashes a kid sometimes gets when he suddenly realizes what it's like to be a genius—even for a second—I ran back to my room, yanked the top sheet off my unmade bed, and returned to the garage. I carefully wrapped the sheet around my decorated tree—again and again. When I finished, the needles had disappeared beneath a blue turban of cotton and polyester. It was an evergreen masquerading as a mummy. No ornaments would fall off now. No needles would be lost. More importantly, no one would know what I was carrying on my bike.

The next moment, I blasted out of our garage and down the street at a fast pedal. Our neighbor, Mrs. Simon, would have needed high-speed camera equipment to spy me from her window. I was a blur of blue.

At that clip, it only took a moment for me to realize I had aerodynamic issues that even NASA couldn't solve. My puny tree had suddenly met a hurricane. It was doing precisely what the chief said trees did—and taught us to do—even when wrapped in a bedsheet. It was bending in the wind. I didn't have a choice but to slow down and grab my tilted passenger with one hand while I steered with the other. This saved it from falling, but it was the end of the blue blur.

I took the route where I was least likely to encounter familiar faces, including my parents. But I still drew my share of looks from curious pedestrians and passing motorists. I also fetched a decent double-take from a man stacking firewood. Kids pointed, too. It's a big deal seeing another kid take a Saturday morning to the edge, but I didn't see anyone I recognized. Not even Gooter.

As expected, no one was around when I reached the lot. Still, I kept my bike helmet on as I unloaded the tree. Beneath the protective bowl of white plastic, I looked like any other kid lacking parental supervision. From my backpack, I removed a bottle of sugar water, setting it on the ground, and then from my bike rack, I untied the key to Christmas tree perpindicularity: the stand. In this case, the large coffee can that my dad had used whenever he changed the oil in the Plymouth. As much coffee as he drank, he would empty a new one in no time.

I worked quickly, first bracing the coffee can with stones so it wouldn't tip. Next, I filled it with sugar water. After unwrapping the sheet, I set the tree in the can and filled it with dirt so the trunk would stand straight. Finally, I inspected the ornaments. With the exception of some flattened paper chains and some tinsel stuck to the sheet, all the trimmings, including the cardboard angel, had survived the bike ride.

The chief's tree, heavy with swaying trinkets, stood at last in the middle of his well-swept campsite. If no one touched it and if the wind didn't blow, it might just stand through Christmas.

As I got on my bike, I turned for one last look. In the wide expanse of the lot, "puny" was truly the right word for it. More than ever, the little tree looked starved of something, but it certainly wasn't ornaments. Maybe it was the ugliest Christmas tree Irene had ever seen. Maybe it wouldn't stay upright for more than a day, but it was there, waiting for him. Like all gifts from the heart, it held a small promise.

That night, my mom prepared her usual Christmas Eve buffet of crab Newburg and Swedish meatballs served in her shiny chafing dishes. I could have managed with a hot dog and some tater tots, but my mom always got fancy on Christmas Eve. At the table, she asked if I had put up my tree.

"Up and decorated," I answered, moving chunks of crab to the edge of my plate.

Irene started to say something, but she stopped herself. With major gift-getting only hours away, she may have decided to be nice to me and not push my buttons. She was really counting on that iPod to be under our tree Christmas morning.

"Where did you put it, son?" my dad asked.

"I donated it to a shelter," I replied, having prepared this truest of answers in advance. Chief Goodyear was in a shelter—his own.

Everyone stopped eating and looked at me. Irene's mouth was open.

"Why ... how thoughtful of you," declared my mom. "I had no idea."

I shoveled in a forkful of rice, as if I enjoyed it, and said, "After you told me about those rescue missions giving away turkey at Thanksgiving, I figured homeless people might want to have a Christmas tree, too."

My mom looked at my dad. She was beaming big-time. My dad disconnected from his plate long enough to keep the ball in play.

"Well, that was a very considerate gesture, Charlie. Good job, son."

Naturally, you can't count on your parents to be satisfied with just the broad brushstrokes. They have to know about the paint under your fingernails, too.

"Which shelter was it, dear?" my mom asked, tilting her head. "The Crossroads?"

I couldn't lie on Christmas Eve, not with the baby Jesus already on his way to the manger, and definitely not over fancy buffet food like this. So I played dumb.

"I don't know its name, Mom," I replied. I looked in her direction, but not at her. "I just saw it from the bus. I think it's new."

My mom considered this response with a thoughtful expression. "That must be the shelter that just opened on Marsh Street," she announced. "I think the Evangelical Mennonites are running it."

I nodded, but I didn't say anything. Undoubtedly, Marsh Street was in the general neighborhood. And Mennonites of any kind were beyond my comment.

"It's important to think of others. Especially this time of

year," said my mom. She turned to Irene and said, "Wasn't that nice of Charlie, Irene?"

Irene swallowed her food and said, "Oh, yes."

The way she said it made me look up. She was staring at me over her glass of cranberry juice. Her eyes had a message. Her next words seemed to speak in code.

"Charlie is very nice to strangers," she lilted. "Everyone says so."

I studied the crab on my plate, trying to disguise a sudden plunge into panic.

Does she know?

My dad said, "We'd do well to be nice to everybody, Irene, whether we know them or not."

Silence unfolded. I waited for Irene to say more. If she knew where my tree had gone and what I had been doing on the lot, now was the moment to tighten the noose.

For some reason, she didn't.

"I suppose," she agreed flatly. Somewhere in one of our closets, an unwrapped iPod was waiting for a nametag. Had Irene decided not to tempt Santa?

As we drove by the lot that night on our way to Mass, I stared at the chief's campsite out the window. There was no point in pretending not to. In the front seat, my dad focused on the road while my mom filled our pledge envelopes with money. Irene was looking out the window, too.

I spied the chief standing close to his grill, a shadowy figure with hands outstretched over a red glow. I thought

I recognized the silhouette of a teakettle on the grill and a ski hat on his head.

The chief's tent, the tires, and the tree were only shadows on the lot. I strained to catch a blink of tinsel or the shimmer off a CD, but I saw only darkness.

Irene suddenly nudged me.

"Don't worry, stupid," she whispered with a tenderness that surprised me. "I won't tell anyone about your ugly tree. Just be nice to me."

That's when I knew my secret was safe—and discovered the high price of a sister's silence.

It snowed that night—only a dusting—but those in our house who had wished for a white Christmas awoke to one. If it hadn't been for the chief sleeping in a tent, I would have wished for it, too. My dad said that the first snow is like a fresh start in life.

That morning, the only start that interested me was starting the Christmas joy. There was the baby Jesus to place in the manger and stockings to empty. Most urgently, there was a pile of gifts under our huge tree, each one waiting to be opened. I didn't believe in Santa anymore, but I still believed you got what you asked for. I also believed in surprises.

I received plenty of both that morning. I made a killing

in the action figure, card warfare, and electronic game departments. Naturally, Irene was happy with her new iPod.

Next came an onslaught of relatives, including several of my cousins with loot of their own. Amid the chaos of company, Christmas dinner, toy talk, and play, the day passed in a blur. Sadly, I didn't give much thought to the chief. I didn't worry about the snow melting on his tent. I didn't regret that he was working at McDonald's. I didn't wonder what he ate for Christmas dinner while I demolished baked ham. I didn't even think about the tree. I guess Irene had been right when she said that I was still a kid.

The day after Christmas, I awoke feeling like I had cheated in catechism class. I decided to make a couple ham sandwiches, pack them in aluminum foil, and run them down to the tent. Even the day after, Christmas ham was still Christmas ham. I also wanted to know if the tree had survived the night.

But my mom announced that we were making an overnight to Thorndale to visit more relatives. What timing! I wanted to complain, but I couldn't say that travel was a terrible imposition on getting ham into the right hands.

In the Roebecker household, kids didn't have votes, so, under protest, I went. But I called Gooter first to find out what he had gotten for Christmas and to tell him I wouldn't be over to play because I was being abducted. He gave me his list, and, except for the clothes, all were quality gifts—including a new bike.

Then he said, "Hey, have you checked out the lot?"

I hesitated for a second, lining up the right words. "I've been too busy," I said.

"That homeless guy put up a tree next to his tent. It's the ugliest tree you've ever seen. And he decorated it, too. You gotta see it. It's creepy looking."

"Really?" I said, not quite speechless.

"Yeah. We drove by yesterday. My mom stopped because she wanted to leave the chief some food. Christmas cookies, I think. And there was this tree. I was going to get down and check it out. I mean, the thing looks like some kid decorated it. But my mom wouldn't let me. She said I had no business there, if you can believe that!"

I believed it. I had no business going to Thorndale, but orders were orders.

"Was the chief there?" I asked. In the background, I heard Gooter's mother telling him to keep it short.

"I didn't see him," he answered, and then his voice dropped. "I told my mother that a crazy dog was tied up there, but she took the cookies to his tent anyway, and when she came back to the car, she said there wasn't any dog. So maybe it ran away or got stolen or run over or something. Hey, I gotta hang up. Check it out when you get back, if it's still there. I don't think it will be, because it's barely standing, apart from being ugly. My mom says Merry Christmas and all that. Bye."

I put down the phone. Gooter had been a gold mine of

information. The puny tree had made it through Christmas day, upright and decorated. The chief had gotten cookies. And now I knew the identity of the other charitable soul. Gooter's mom.

Two days later, we were back from Thorndale. It hadn't snowed while we were gone, which was good news for the chief. But, as soon we hit town, Irene asked if we could go to McDonald's for lunch.

She didn't just ask. She begged.

"Oh, please, Daddy. Just this once," she pleaded in her drama queen voice. It was pitiful.

I thought my dad would hold fast to his principles, wanting to keep his perfect record intact. But in case he wavered, I was quick to side with reason.

"Count me out. I'm not hungry," I said from the backseat. That drew silence, so I added, "Anyway, it's not good to eat too much fast food."

That was a quote from someone who actually worked at McDonald's, but I couldn't cite the source. My dad smiled at me through the rearview mirror, and that's when I realized he was going to compromise.

"I'll tell you what," he announced. "We'll use the drive-through. How's that? Then I don't have to go inside."

I couldn't believe what Irene did next. She released her

seat belt, and she reached across the front seat to hug my dad from behind. We never unbuckled while the Plymouth was in motion, and we never distracted Dad while he was behind the wheel. I waited for him to give the command to cease, desist, and buckle up, but he went along with the moment. He took his eyes off the road long enough to peck Irene on the cheek. My dad was definitely slipping. I figured it must be the holidays.

"Maybe I'll have a burger, too," he said.

"And I'll order a salad," my mom added.

"I'm going to have a spicy chicken sandwich with fries," declared Irene.

"Are you sure don't want something, Charlie?" my dad asked.

"I'm good," I answered grimly.

Mortified was more like it. Adding my order to the list would keep us parked outside McDonald's that much longer. And that would increase the chances of the chief spotting me. It would be my luck he was working the lunch hour at the drive-through window.

I imagined him poking his friendly face through the sliding glass, scanning the occupants of our minivan until he recognized me.

"Hey, Charlie, is that you?" Then he'd acknowledge my parents' dumbfounded looks with, "Hi there, folks. I'm Bill, a friend of your son. He's been keeping an eye on Pipe for me. Haven't you, Charlie?"

Their perplexed faces would ask, "Pipe? A pipe? Who? What was that?"

Or the nightmare might deepen. He would say, "Hey, Charlie, guess what? Someone brought a decorated Christmas tree to the lot."

I quickly scanned the car for something to hide behind. A two-page spread from our local paper, preferably the sports section, would have provided good camouflage, but the best cover I could find was a shabby-looking Christmas pageant program left in the car from the previous Sunday. It wasn't something I could disappear behind—a Hallmark card was bigger—but it would have to do.

As we pulled into the drive-through and approached the menu board, I shriveled into the far corner of our rearmost seat. The pageant program was touching my nose.

A male voice took our order. With the microphone crackle in the background, I couldn't tell if it was the chief.

My dad eased the Plymouth forward to the pay window. I shifted my weight, doing my best to disappear into the cup holder on my door. Words from the pageant program hugged my eyelashes.

"Joseph of Arimathea played by Jason Huo," I read, practically smelling the ink.

The pay window opened.

"That will be $16.50, please," chirped a young man's voice.

I peered over the program. My mom was handing money

to my dad. From the window, a pale, hairless hand took it. Definitely no hand belonging to the chief. So far, so good.

We edged forward to the pickup window. Again, I tried to make myself disappear. I had met the chief at the pickup window before. Its wide glass opened into the frantic, employee-crowded McKitchen where practically anyone inside could see into the car. If I were to be spotted, it would be here.

I turned and pretended to be fascinated by the door lock. The pageant program was stuck to my face. Then I heard the glass windows slide open.

"Here we go," announced a peppy accent.

Yes. A girl!

At the sound of paper bags stretching around hot food, I began to relax. The smell of french fries flooded our car.

"And here are your drinks," said the girl.

My dad took his time positioning the cups. He may not have set a foot inside the Golden Arches, but he was clocking plenty of overtime outside them.

I wanted to nudge the Plymouth forward and make that window disappear behind us, when out of the corner of my eye, I saw my dad popping a fry into his mouth.

Double time, Captain! March!

"Is there ketchup in the bag?" asked my mom.

This was no time to scream, but I wanted to. I could only hide and hope the chief wasn't hovering in the background with ketchup ready. My face was hot. For a moment,

IV

THE NEXT MORNING, I took three, foil-wrapped ham sandwiches to the lot, but as soon as I reached Hildreth's, I saw I was too late. No grill. No tires. No tent. The chief had left.

He had been gone for at least a day, maybe more. Trash had blown back onto the lot. The campsite wasn't swept. My mortification at McDonald's had been for nothing.

The lot was vacant except for the tree. My tree ... the chief's tree ... the ugliest Christmas tree, if you believed Irene and Gooter. It was still standing, but the decorations were gone. Only the tinsel was left.

The sight left me with a strange kind of emptiness, as if something inside me had gone missing. I had felt this way once before, when our family dog had come down with leukemia, and my dad had taken him to the vet to be put asleep. It was that kind of emptiness. The chief had left without a good-bye, and I had never gotten a chance to wish him Merry Christmas or Happy New Year. I hadn't even wished him a good life, a better life. Sometimes, you can do only small things to fix a big problem.

When I arrived at the tree, I noticed something white stuck between the pine boughs. At first, I thought it was a piece of paper blown there by the wind, but then I saw handwriting and recognized the shape. It was an envelope.

I pulled it from the branches and read, "To Whomever Finds This."

The words were written across the front in dark ink. I flipped the envelope over. The flap was sealed.

My first thought was, not everyone uses "whomever" in our town.

Only those people who knew if it was good grammar, and I was not one of them. My second thought was a sixth-grade grasp of the obvious: *I, Charlie Roebecker, am the first "whomever" on the lot to find it!*

It was like a message in a bottle, waiting for me to come ashore. I fingered the flap, wondering if I should open it here. It seemed a strange business leaving behind an envelope for a whomever the writer would never know.

My gaze dropped to the tree. It looked shorter and punier. Without ornaments, it was scrawnier than ever. The tinsel only made it look more lonesome. I followed its crooked trunk to the ground, looking for my dad's coffee can—the one I had left as a tree stand—but it was missing. The big stones I had positioned there to brace it were gone, too. I stepped back, wondering how the tree was standing without them. Its trunk seemed to disappear into the ground.

Then I saw that it did disappear into the ground. The trunk was buried in the dirt! Now I understood why the tree looked shorter. The chief had planted it.

"No way!" I exclaimed, immediately dropping to my knees for a closer look.

But planted the Puny was, its trunk buried up to the lowest boughs in the lot's stony dirt. The earth around it had been molded into a trough and then tightly packed. What's more, the soil was wet. The chief had watered the tree, too!

I shook my head in disbelief. It seemed like a lot of work for nothing. A Christmas tree couldn't grow after it was cut. It didn't have roots!

For as long as I could remember, I had watched our own Christmas trees dry up in the backyard after their unceremonious removal from our living room. I watched their needles turn orange-brown while we waited for the tree disposal man and his wood-chipping machine to arrive in our neighborhood. Some things you just knew in this life—your name, the color of your mother's eyes, and what happened to a Christmas tree after Christmas.

I got to my feet and pulled on one of the boughs, half expecting to see the tree tip over. Surprisingly, it resisted. It might have been my imagination, but the Puny seemed to pull back.

I wondered if the chief had decided to apply his arborist's skills to the scrawny pine or if he simply had needed an empty coffee can for the trip. I looked at the unopened note in my hand, wondering if the answer was inside.

Slipping a fingernail under the flap, I tore it open and removed a folded piece of paper that I immediately recognized. It was the sign I had left in his tent before Thanksgiving, the one advertising the Safe Harbor Hospitality House lunch. On the blank side, a handwritten note filled the entire page. I stood next to the tree and read it:

If you are who I think you are, I have so many things I want to say beyond thank you. But I only have one side of this paper, so here's the short list. The sleeping bag was warm, and that sweater was priceless. (I love blue elephants.) The flashlight let me read, while the sewing kit saved my shorts. The oatmeal was delicious, those nuts were a treat, and I'm still taking the vitamins. That may be why I haven't gotten sick. Did you bring those cookies, too? As for our tree, it is the most beautiful Christmas tree anywhere and the most originally decorated. The angel is lovely. I've kept the trimmings for Christmases to come, but I've returned the little pine to the ground, where all trees belong. It seems fair that if I was given the opportunity to begin a new life after tough times, then why shouldn't it? Something tells me it will do well with you nearby. Water it, Charlie, when you can. (But no sugar!) You, too, will do well, wherever you end up belonging.

My jaw dropped. I didn't quite believe what I had read until I read it again. But there it was.

"Water it, Charlie, when you can."

So he knew! Even about the sugar.

After all my precautions, he had found out somehow. Had he seen me? Had I left some clue? Had somebody told him? Gooter's mom?

I folded the note and started to put it in my pocket when I noticed handwriting at the bottom of the printed side. It was penned in the same ink.

PS: Be nice to your sister. She's not as bad as you think. In fact, she is a lot like you. She brought the socks and cat food. Mr. Hildreth saw you both.

Bill

That was one too many surprises for a kid just getting over Christmas.

Mr. Hildreth a spy? Irene a charitable soul? What next? A scrawny Christmas tree sprouting roots?

I stared at the note, amazed at how complicated a sister could be. She had called the chief creepy. She had wanted to bring the police. She had refused to pray for him. Then she had brought him socks. A contradiction seemed to be there, but it did explain why she had kept my secret. Now I'd have to keep hers. Helping the chief had become *our* secret.

I thought about saying something to her to let her know I knew. I wanted her to see that I wasn't as dumb as she thought I was, but that wouldn't have been nice. Irene had told me to be nice to her, and the chief had written the same. I didn't have any choice now but to try.

After refolding the note, I slipped it into my jacket pocket. Something inside me felt stretched and rubbery. It wasn't an awful feeling or even a nice one. Just new.

Then I walked home.

It snowed four inches that night—the wet, snowball-making kind of snow. The next morning, Gooter called.

"Guess what?" he blurted.

"The chief's gone," I replied.

"You know the … huh? Who told you?"

"I went to Hildreth's."

"Really? My mom just got back from leaving him fudge. Make that not leaving him fudge. She said the lot was empty. Let's go build a fort."

"Meet you there," I said, knowing I didn't have a choice. If the snow hadn't messed with the Puny, Gooter would.

I arrived first and saw that it was still standing. Being scrawny had its advantages in a snowstorm; there was hardly any tree for the snow to stick to.

Gooter showed up wearing his new winter boots.

He said, "Hey, there's that ugly tree I told you about. Isn't it pitiful?"

I was ready. "Yeah," I said. "I guess the chief left it for us."

Gooter looked at me and said, "What do you mean?"

"To take care of," I replied.

Now Gooter really looked at me.

"What are you talking about? It's dead. It doesn't even belong here. I say we pull it up."

"That's what homeless people do, Gooter."

"What?"

"They leave something behind."

"Get out!"

"It's like a gift for the people who help them when they're homeless—people like your mom who give them stuff."

Gooter stared at me. "You're kidding, right?"

I smiled and said, "Yeah, but I think we ought to leave it, just in case."

Sometimes a friend needs help to see the right path.

"It'll dry up anyway," argued Gooter as we headed to the chief's abandoned campsite.

"I know," I said. "But does that mean we should knock it down?"

We stared at the Puny. Gooter didn't answer. Instead he pulled on a bough, bending the trunk toward him. I watched and held my breath.

"It's going to be in the way when we play," he said, suddenly letting go.

"Maybe," I answered, watching the tree snap back and stand straight again. "But no one is playing ball right now, so what's the big deal?"

Gooter scooped a handful of snow, molded it, and moved away from me.

"I suppose," he said.

"I'd feel better if we just let it fall by itself. Let nature do it."

"Charlie, have you been talking to the reverend or someone? You seem awful worried about doing the right thing."

"No," I replied. "I just think that if people leave something behind and we don't know why, we better not mess with it."

"Okay. You're getting too complicated. Leave the stupid tree. I don't care."

Then Gooter threw a snowball at me, hard.

"Hey, no fair!"

"What do you mean no one is playing ball?" he said, grabbing another handful and swiftly making a new one. "Catch!"

I dodged it, scooped snow, made a quick one, and then unloaded. Both of us moved away from the tree, making war and laughing.

Later, we rolled snow boulders and circled them into a

fort. I had the idea to build it around the tree, and Gooter quickly agreed.

"Yeah. So no one can see how ugly it is."

And that's how we left the chief's tree—standing inside a snow fort, safe and unseen.

We took down our own tree, Irene's tree, on Epiphany. It was the same day I moved the magi in our crèche into the final position next to the baby Jesus who lay inside that poor-looking stable. Even back then, accommodations for the homeless weren't much to look at.

A week later, the tree-chipper man stopped in our neighborhood. He dragged the tall Douglas fir to the street and pushed it into the wide mouth of his whirring machine.

I thought of the chief as I watched the tree get chewed into confetti, and I wondered what he would have said. Naturally, I found myself thinking a lot about him in those first weeks. I wondered if he had made it to Florida with Pipe. I wondered if he had found a job and a home. I wondered if he would plant old Christmas trees there, too.

A thaw in January melted our snow fort, making the chief's tree a public spectacle again. Still, no one but me paid any attention to it from the bus. Not even Gooter was interested. Turning twelve that month had taken over his brain. All he could talk about was becoming a teenager. It was awful.

I knew the melting snow would give the tree plenty of water, but when I finally got to the lot, I saw that the little pine might as well have been standing in the middle of a desert. The Puny was drying up just like Christmas trees are supposed to. Its needles were turning rusty and barely hanging on. When I touched one of the boughs, a whole handful fell to ground. Nature may be slower than a chipper, but it gets the job done.

The chief had talked about trees being tough and teaching us about surviving. He might have been right about the rooted ones, but a planted Christmas tree was far from that school.

Still, you had to give the Puny credit for standing up. When the weather warmed in February and we didn't get any rain, I did my duty. Every Saturday, I took a jug of sugar-free tap water to the lot and poured it on the little tree. I did it because the chief had asked me to do it, not because I expected the scrawny pine to rise from the tree grave. When one jug didn't seem enough, I packed more dirt around the chief's trough to make the dike higher so I could add two jugs.

By then, not a needle was on it. The Puny had turned into a tree skeleton—one that hardly cast a shadow. Yet somehow it managed to stay upright. Maybe the chief had done something tricky underground, a secret only arborists knew. Defiantly, it braved a freak blizzard in early March. A windy St. Patrick's Day came and went. Still it stood. April brought rain and then mud. Grass started sprouting in the lot.

In May, the ground was dry enough to start baseball. So

it was no surprise when Gooter called to say the boys were meeting at Hildreth's to play. As soon as we got there, kids wanted to pull up the tree to clear the outfield. The general opinion was that the little tree was the ugliest dead tree on the planet.

Fortunately, it lined up perfectly with first base and home plate. When I suggested using it to mark our right field foul line, everyone rushed to verify the geometry, and then agreed.

Gooter was the first to yell, "Let's play ball!"

That summer, the chief's tree miraculously escaped annihilation. Somehow, it didn't get run over in our chase for pop flies or knocked down by our diving catches. Even hard ground balls bouncing foul didn't touch it.

Then school started again, and I didn't go to the lot. Sometimes I looked out the bus window when we passed it. Sometimes I even noticed the tree, but I wasn't thinking about it anymore. I guess turning twelve does that. A dead Christmas tree left in a vacant lot by a homeless man sort of loses importance. I hardly thought about the chief, either.

When the afternoons turned cool and the leaves started to change color, we returned to the lot again to play soccer. This time, the tree became our corner marker. Amazingly, it stood in the perfect spot.

As it turned out, the spot was perfect for another reason. If it hadn't stood where it did, then Ricky Martinez, our right forward and a kid with a keen eye for dropped pocket change, wouldn't have yelled, "Hey, come look at this!" one Saturday

as he positioned the ball for a corner kick next to the tree. No one else would have noticed.

We gathered around him, following the tip of his finger to where it pointed at the tree. All of us stared. Gooter and I dropped our jaws. Ricky was pointing to green. The tree bough closest to the ground was green! Pine tree green!

The chief's Christmas tree had baby needles.

"What the ...!" blurted Gooter, his eyes wide.

I stared, not quite believing it either. Then I took one of the upper boughs between my fingers and bent it. Instead of snapping, it wrapped around my knuckle. It was green on the inside, too.

"Good thing we didn't pull it up," Gooter said.

Everyone moved away. Ricky kicked the ball, and play resumed.

But I stayed near the tree, resisting the urge to jump up and down. I felt like wrapping my arms around the tiny pine and shouting to the sky. But that would have looked funny in the middle of a soccer game. How crazy was a kid supposed to get over a Christmas tree that managed to rise from the dead?

Had that second jug of tap water saved it? Had leaving out the sugar helped? Had the hands of an arborist somehow made a difference? Or had nature pulled it off on its own?

While most trees were ready to sleep for the winter, the ugly little pine had woken up.

What a time to come back to life.

"C'mon, Roebecker!" shouted Gooter. "Quit playing with the stupid tree."

I turned to look at them. Like me, they were young and careless. I couldn't tell them I preferred the company I was keeping. I couldn't say I was standing next to a phenomenon, one for the record books. I couldn't tell them that Chief Goodyear, the homeless arborist who had camped where we were playing, had been right. Trees are tough.

I couldn't. So I ran into the game and kicked the ball.

Within a month, the tree was green again. Green, scrawny, and, according to Gooter, still ugly. But I didn't care. The teaching had begun. The chief might as well have said, "Charlie, welcome to tree school." Besides, I had been right from the start. You only needed imagination to see what this tree might become.

Our soccer games and my visits to Hildreth's lot ended when the ground froze and an early snow fell. Even though I hadn't figured out how trees get by when the dirt freezes around them, I didn't worry about the little pine. I knew it would survive.

Christmas came. My dad drove Irene and me to Mr. Paulson's tent for the annual tree picking. Again, Irene chose a Douglas fir fit for the White House. It wasn't as tall as last year's, but it was horribly perfect. This time, I didn't make any comments about clones or steroids. I was nice. And she was nice back.

"Charlie, I want you to help me decorate it this year," she declared.

She actually said my name.

"Aren't you going to get one, too?" my father asked, nodding toward the corner where all the rejects stood.

"Yeah, Charlie, I've got some dandy lop-offs," agreed Mr. Paulson. "Won't charge ya."

I shook my head and said, "Thanks. I'm not doing a tree this year."

My dad might have thought I had lost my charitable side, but I hadn't. I just hadn't seen a homeless man camped out in a vacant lot in our town.

As usual, my mom and I set up the crèche, and she talked about miracles. When she asked me if I believed in them, I said I wanted to. Obviously, I kept the miraculous comeback of the tree at Hildreth's to myself. I wasn't sure if it was a miracle.

I thought a lot about the chief that Christmas. There were reports on the TV about the hurricane people. Some were going home, rebuilding, starting over, and spending their first Christmas in new houses. I wondered if the chief was among them. I watched the pictures on the news, looking for him, trying to pick out a man with a dog. But I never saw him. I would never know if he went back or if he found work in Florida helping knocked-over trees stand straight again.

The pine tree on Hildreth's lot grew the next year. It grew greener, taller, and fuller. Most of the boys agreed that it wasn't quite as ugly as the year before.

Even though I didn't know it then, it would eventually grow so much that it would get in the way of the games we played. Its branches would interfere with corner kicks. Its piney top would knock fair balls foul. It would force us to retreat to real ball fields. By then, we would be big kids.

Mr. Hildreth eventually hung Christmas lights on it when the holidays arrived, running an extension cord from his store. His lot became our local Rockefeller Center at Christmas. Mr. Hildreth's tree became another holiday landmark, just like the sixteen thousand lights decorating the front of Billy Wetmore's house.

Eventually, the tree I had brought and the chief had planted grew into the tallest, fullest pine tree in the neighborhood. Eventually, no one noticed the crooked trunk beneath the thick evergreen boughs. No one remembered its missing top. Eventually, people who were new to town would stare and exclaim, "Look at that tree! Isn't it beautiful?"

And that's the truth. I don't overdo my adjectives.

Miracles sometimes occur,
but one has to work terribly hard for them.

—Chaim Weizmann

Now Available as a Sentry Audio Book

Sentry Books™

Visit us at www.sentryaudio.com